Books by Matt Christopher

Sports Stories

THE LUCKY BASEBALL BAT
BASEBALL PALS
BASKETBALL SPARKPLUG
TWO STRIKES ON JOHNNY
LITTLE LEFTY
TOUCHDOWN FOR TOMMY
LONG STRETCH AT FIRST BASE
BREAK FOR THE BASKET
TALL MAN IN THE PIVOT
CHALLENGE AT SECOND BASE
CRACKERJACK HALFBACK
BASEBALL FLYHAWK
SINK IT, RUSTY
CATCHER WITH A GLASS ARM
WINGMAN ON ICE
TOO HOT TO HANDLE
THE COUNTERFEIT TACKLE
THE RELUCTANT PITCHER
LONG SHOT FOR PAUL
MIRACLE AT THE PLATE

THE TEAM THAT COULDN'T LOSE
THE YEAR MOM WON THE PENNANT
THE BASKET COUNTS
HARD DRIVE TO SHORT
CATCH THAT PASS!
SHORTSTOP FROM TOKYO
LUCKY SEVEN
JOHNNY LONG LEGS
LOOK WHO'S PLAYING FIRST BASE
TOUGH TO TACKLE
THE KID WHO ONLY HIT HOMERS
FACE-OFF
MYSTERY COACH
ICE MAGIC
NO ARM IN LEFT FIELD
JINX GLOVE
FRONT COURT HEX

Animal Stories

DESPERATE SEARCH
STRANDED

FRONT
COURT
HEX

FRONT COURT HEX

by

Matt Christopher

Illustrated by Byron Goto

Little, Brown and Company
Boston　　　　*Toronto*

FIRST EDITION

T 09/74

Library of Congress Cataloging in Publication Data

Christopher, Matthew F
  Front court hex.

  [1. Basketball--Fiction. 2. Witches--Fiction]
I. Goto, Byron, illus. II. Title.
PZ7.C458Fr [Fic] 74-1143
ISBN 0-316-13920-3

*Published simultaneously in Canada
by Little, Brown & Company (Canada) Limited*

PRINTED IN THE UNITED STATES OF AMERICA

to Marty, Margaret and Michael

FRONT
COURT
HEX

1

HOW COULD LAST YEAR'S basketball star have played two games this year so far and not have scored a point?

Jerry Steele looked up at the ceiling. Had he really played those two games so badly? Perhaps it was only a dream. But the longer he stared the more certain he was that the games really had been played.

His mother's voice boomed from the kitchen for the third time. "Jerry! Will you *please* get up? It's getting late!"

Grumbling an unintelligible answer, he rolled out of bed, yanked out clean underclothes from the dresser drawer and began to dress.

Five minutes later he was sitting at the kitchen table eating his breakfast. His mother, whose light brown hair lay in soft curls across her shoulders, shook her head and sighed.

"Jerry," she said, "sometimes you amaze me how quickly you can get ready."

He grinned. "The secret word is 'late,' Mom. The minute I heard that — *zap!* — I moved like Batman."

"I wish you'd move with half that speed when I ask you to take out the garbage, or shovel snow off the sidewalk," she said. "Your Dad had to do both of those chores yesterday, and it was your job."

"Aw, Ma! I just forgot!" He chomped

4

on his toast without looking at her, knowing that she was right. But there was something about small jobs around the house that made him ignore them, even though he knew they had to be done. His father did the bigger jobs, like repairing leaks in the plumbing or fixing the roof; Jerry was expected to help with the smaller ones.

"Well, make sure you don't forget again, young man," said his mother as she stacked the breakfast dishes in the sink.

Jerry nodded. After he finished breakfast he put on his jacket, gathered up his books, and headed for the door. "See ya later, Mom," he said. He kissed her on the cheek and left.

The air was nippy, biting at Jerry's face as he headed for school four blocks away. It was December, and a soft white blanket

6

of snow covered the roofs, the streets, and the sidewalks in the small town of Spitford, huddled at the foot of the Catskill Mountains.

A new thought suddenly troubled him. He remembered the book report he had asked Ronnie Malone to do for him because he hadn't had time to do it himself. Well, *time* wasn't quite the word. He had as much time as anyone else in the class. He just didn't want to *take* it, that was all. And he assumed, Ronnie, being his best friend would do it.

"Don't expect me to do it all the time, Jerry," Ronnie had said. "If Miss Clarey finds out she'll never trust either one of us again."

"Don't worry, she won't find out," Jerry had answered.

He met Ronnie in the locker room. The

tall, red-headed boy, in blue pants and white pullover, passed a couple of folded sheets of paper to Jerry and said, "Make sure you copy it over."

"Don't worry," Jerry replied. "Think I'm stupid? Don't answer that!"

He thanked Ronnie. Later, in study hall, he copied over the report. With every word he wrote he felt a sense of guilt. He was tempted to throw the paper away and start one of his own, but the thought that the report was already completed won him over. His forehead beaded with sweat, he finished copying it, tore up the original, and tossed the pieces into a wastebasket.

That afternoon he handed the report in, hoping that Miss Clarey didn't notice his shaking hand.

That night the game against the Foxfires started at 6:30 in the school gym. All the players were there at 6:00 warming up. The Chariots, for whom Jerry played guard, wore maroon, white-trimmed uniforms. The Foxfires wore scarlet.

"How many shots are you going to miss tonight, Jerry?" somebody asked.

Jerry looked around at the tall, blond boy behind him. Freddie Pearse was the Chariots' center. Although he was never a close friend of Jerry's, that wisecrack made him less a friend now. The fact that Jerry had played two games without scoring a single point hadn't set well with Freddie either.

Jerry shrugged. "Let's wait and see," he said.

Each Chariot took his turn shooting at the basket. When Jerry's turn came, he ran in toward the basket, caught the toss from the man in the other line, jumped up and laid it in.

"Hey, man!" shouted Chuck Metz, the team's forward and Freddie Pearse's pal. "He made it!"

"Sure, but wait till the game starts," said Freddie. "He'll choke up."

Jerry's face turned cherry red as he tried to ignore the center's sarcasm. Freddie was getting to be too much.

Game time came and the Chariots huddled around Coach Dick Stull, a tall, broad-shouldered man with black hair and long sideburns.

"The big thing on defense is to play your man," he reminded them. "Keep between him and the ball and be careful not to foul. Last Thursday the Pilots picked up eight points on us on fouls alone, so

10

let's cut that figure down. Jerry, you're starting again. You didn't score a single point in the first two games, so I'm sure you're ready to bust loose. Okay, let's go."

They broke out of the huddle and ran to their positions on the court, Ronnie and Chuck at forward, Freddie at center, Lin Foo and Jerry at guard. Jumping center for the Foxfires was Eddie Reed, a tall, rangy kid with glasses. A chorus of yells and whistles exploded from the fans in the bleachers.

The referee's whistle shrilled, the ball went up, the centers jumped. Freddie tapped the ball to Chuck. Chuck caught it and dribbled down the sideline. The Foxfire guarding him bolted in front of him, arms reaching for the ball, and Chuck passed it to Ronnie. Ronnie turned, faked

11

a throw that fooled his guard, then shot. The ball sank through the hoop without touching the rim.

The Chariot fans went wild. Jerry, watching both his man and the Foxfire taking out the ball, kicked out his right foot as he saw the bounce coming. The ball ricocheted up, he caught it, and bolted down the court. Seconds later his man was in front of him, arms beating the air. Jerry passed to Chuck, then broke for the basket. During that moment while Jerry was in the clear, Chuck passed him the ball and up he went with it.

The ball hit the boards, bounded against the rim — and off!

"Ohhhh, no!" groaned the Chariot fans.

"Jeepers, Jerry!" grumbled a voice Jerry recognized as Freddie Pearse's. "You couldn't make a shot if you were standing

over the basket! What's with you, anyway?"

I don't know, Jerry wanted to say. *I just
don't know.*

2

A FOXFIRE CAUGHT A REBOUND, passed to a teammate, who dribbled down the court, no one in front of him. No one for a while, that is, for just as he crossed the center line Jerry reached him and stole the ball.

Jerry dribbled to the sideline, two Foxfires after him, and shot a pass to Ronnie. Ronnie moved the ball halfway down the front court and was instantly double-teamed. He leaped and passed to Freddie who came to a dead stop near the foul line and took a shot. The ball bounced

14

against the boards and into the net.

"Nice steal, Jerry!" yelled a fan, and Jerry recognized his father's voice. He smiled warmly. His father and mother, his best rooters, never missed a game if they could help it.

Again the Foxfires took out the ball. This time the pass to a teammate was good. He dribbled the ball down the court and passed it to a man in a corner. The man shot and hit for two points.

Jerry took out the ball for the Chariots, bounce passing it to Ronnie who dribbled it upcourt. A Foxfire threatened to take the ball from him and he passed to Freddie. The tall center was smothered instantly, the ball slipping out of his hands and rolling free. Jerry and a Foxfire bolted after it. Jerry, reaching it first, grabbed it up, dribbled to a corner, saw no one free to pass to, and took a set. The ball hit the rim, bounded up high, came down and hit the rim again. Jerry rushed in for the rebound, caught it, jumped for the lay-up and missed.

Again he got the rebound, yanking it out of a Foxfire's hands. But this time he didn't shoot. Panting breathlessly, sweat rolling down his cheeks, he passed off to Ronnie as he heard Freddie's voice ringing in his ears, "Pass it, will you? Your shots are bad, man!"

The whistle shrilled for a jump ball as a Foxfire trapped the ball in Ronnie's hand.

A sub rushed in, pointed at Jerry and Jerry went out, wiping the sweat off his forehead.

"I just can't understand it, Coach," he said, grabbing a towel and drying his face. "The ball just won't go in for me."

16

"I can't understand it, either, Jerry," Coach Stull admitted. "That corner shot looked sure to drop in, and at the last second it looked as if somebody had pulled it away with a string. The same thing happened with that lay-up. No reason why it should've bounced way off the boards like it did, but it did. I guess it's the breaks. Anyway, you're doing fine in defense and I want you to rest a while."

Jerry tossed the towel back to Mickey Ross, the small, dark-haired manager, and sat down. *Yes,* he thought, *it's a good thing I'm doing all right in defense, otherwise I'd be sitting on the bench most of the time.*

The Foxfires held a two-point lead when the quarter ended, and were ahead by six points at the middle of the second quarter.

17

"Okay, Jerry, take Manny's place," Coach Stull said.

Jerry reported to the scorekeeper and went in when a jump ball was called between Lin Foo and a Foxfire guard. Manny Lucas, the sub, went out. Although his man had scored five points against him and none against Jerry, Manny looked disappointed that the coach yanked him.

Lin got the tap off to Chuck Metz, who quickly passed to Freddie. Freddie dribbled downcourt, stopped as he was double-teamed, and drew a whistle when he dragged his pivot foot. He glared at the ref, but gave the ball up without saying a word.

The Foxfires took it out, and in three passes scored a basket to put them eight points ahead.

"Jerry, get in there!" Coach Stull shouted from the sideline.

Jerry frowned at him. *Get in there? I can't be all over the place at once, Coach!*

He succeeded in pulling down a rebound after a miss under the Chariot basket, and brought the ball upcourt. A Foxfire sneaked up unexpectedly beside him and smacked the ball out of his hand. Jerry exploded into fast action, bolting after the ball to get it back. His charge knocked down the Foxfire. A whistle shrilled, and Freddie Pearse yelled, "Watch it, Jerry! This isn't a football game!"

The Foxfire was given a free throw, and sank it. Foxfires 22, Chariots 13.

Still glum over his carelessness, Jerry tossed the ball from out-of-bounds to Ronnie and froze on the spot as he saw a scarlet uniform sweep in front of the red-headed forward, snare the pass, and dribble it downcourt.

"Jerry!" a voice yelled disgustedly, and Jerry realized that someone else had now joined forces against him — Ronnie Malone, his best friend.

For an instant they stared at each other. Then they moved together, sprinting after the dribbler.

"Didn't you see him coming?" Ronnie asked.

"I wouldn't have thrown it to you if I had, would I?" Jerry answered.

"Stop arguing out there and go after that ball!" Coach Stull's voice boomed.

The Foxfire was stopped by Lin Foo, who nearly stole the ball back from him. The Foxfire passed to a teammate. The teammate faked a shot, then lost the

ball to Jerry, who knocked it out of his hands. Jerry dribbled the ball back up-court. Finding himself all alone as he crossed the center line, he sped on to the basket, feeling certain that he couldn't miss now.

He leaped, laid the ball against the boards and feeling sure of himself, ran onto the stage without waiting to see if the ball sank into the net. At the same time a yell rose from the Chariot fans, telling him that he had finally —

Suddenly the yell changed to a surprised groan! *Oh, no!* Jerry thought.

He saw Foxfires and Chariots running in toward the basket, and knew that the easy lay-up shot had missed.

It's impossible! he thought. *That shot was perfect!*

The horn blew, ending the first half.

3

I DON'T KNOW, RONNIE," Jerry said. "Something's sure funny about my missing the basket every time. I *feel* it."

Jerry and Ronnie were in the locker room, near a corner where they couldn't be overheard. The other players sat by themselves, resting for the start of the second half.

"You're just off," Ronnie said. "Anybody could be off sometime. Even me."

He laughed, and Jerry knew that Ronnie was only trying to make him feel better. But not even a good joke could shake him loose from what bothered him now.

"Maybe you're being jinxed," Ronnie said, and laughed again.

Jerry looked at him seriously. "You know — that's exactly how I feel."

"Yeah. Me, too," said Ronnie, and started to walk away.

"Hey! Where are you going?"

"To comb my hair," replied Ronnie.

Jerry watched him open a locker and start combing his hair as he stood in front of a small mirror fastened to the inside of the locker door.

"Red is beautiful," Freddie Pearse said, and a chorus of laughter erupted from the boys. It didn't bother Ronnie, who kept on combing his hair as if he hadn't heard a word.

A few minutes later Coach Stull talked to them, advising them about "better man-

24

to-man defense" and getting "closer to the basket before you shoot," then ordered them upstairs. After both teams had their warm-ups, the second half began. Jerry was surprised that he was starting. Apparently the coach had approved of his performance during the first half.

The first two minutes went by scoreless, neither team approaching its basket close enough to chance a shot. Then Jerry suddenly cut loose, breaking for the basket after a quick pass from Ronnie.

But he didn't shoot. He wasn't going to risk missing a basket again no matter how easy a shot he had. He saw Freddie break away from his guard, and bounced the ball to him. Freddie caught it, went up and sank it for two points.

"Nice play, Jerry!" yelled his favorite fan, his father.

"I'll go along with that," Freddie laughed as they ran back up the court.

"With what?" Jerry asked.

"With that 'nice play' stuff. As long as you don't shoot, you do okay."

"Thanks," said Jerry coolly. Even if he failed with his shots he didn't intend to give up trying altogether. He enjoyed shooting. Scoring points now and then builds up a guy's confidence. It helped the team to win, too.

Jerry kept close guard of his man as the Foxfires moved the ball upcourt. Just over the center line Ronnie pressed the ball handler, forcing him to pass. The throw was poor, and Lin Foo intercepted it, rushing downcourt as fast as he could dribble. Ronnie and a Foxfire ran with him, one on either side. As the Foxfire threatened to stop Lin, the boy flipped

26

the ball to Ronnie. In one sweeping motion, Ronnie caught the pass, jumped and laid it in for two points. Foxfires 22, Chariots 17.

Both coaches sent in subs, and then Freddie Pearse really got hot. He sank four baskets in succession and a foul shot for nine points to the Foxfires' two, making the score Foxfires 24, Chariots 26. The Chariot fans yelled their appreciation, and Jerry saw a smile play at the corners of Freddie's mouth.

Last season things were different. It was *he* who had sunk them one after another. *He* whom the fans had cheered. What was he doing this season that could be so wrong? Why couldn't he even get that first basket? You would think that something was deliberately keeping him from getting it.

Both teams fired in more baskets, and by the end of the third quarter the score was Foxfires 31, Chariots 34.

Coach Stull talked to his charges during the brief intermission, urging them to play "tight ball" during the last quarter. "We're in the lead so let's keep it that way," he said. "Make sure of your passes and don't take any long shots. Freddie has been shooting great this second half, so keep feeding him. If he gets double-teamed, feed Ronnie, or take a shot yourselves. I want you to remember that too, Jerry. The Foxfires must think by now that you're not a shooter, so fool them. Drop in a couple. You're due."

Soft laughter trickled from the players as all eyes turned to Jerry. His face got hot as he found himself the center of attention.

The horn sounded, announcing the beginning of the fourth and last quarter, and Jerry found himself walking out onto the court with Freddie.

"Sure, drop in a couple, Jerry." The tall center laughed. "That wouldn't fool only them. It would fool everybody!"

Jerry found himself becoming blindly angry with Freddie. He wanted to hit him, and only the knowledge that fans were watching stopped him.

The Foxfires took the tap and moved with renewed energy, passing the ball swiftly and accurately in a zigzag pattern up the court. The Chariots seemed dazed at what was going on and suddenly the Foxfires had scored again. 33 – 34.

Chariots' ball. They passed it upcourt, then back and forth to each other as they tried to maneuver it closer to the basket.

Then — an interception! The Foxfires took the ball down to their end of the court and in two passes they scored again. 35 – 34! They were ahead!

"C'mon, you guys!" Freddie yelled. "Let's stop 'em!"

They didn't. The Foxfires dumped in more baskets, raising their score to 43. Twice Jerry had stolen the ball from a Foxfire. Three times he had intercepted passes. But his efforts weren't enough to stop the rolling Foxfires.

The Chariots called time, and once again Coach Stull talked to his charges. "You're too tight, guys. You've got your minds made up that they're going to win, and you're letting them do it. Sure you're playing hard, but you're going about it the wrong way. *Think* when you've got the ball. Hold it for a second before you get

30

rid of it. You can do it. I know you can."

They went out and began playing a different game, a better game. Their passes were accurate, their shots better timed. The gap closed on the score. The minutes became seconds. Fifty-nine . . . fifty-eight . . . fifty-seven . . .

The Foxfires dumped in a shot, then the Chariots dumped in one. With fifteen seconds to go the Foxfires were leading 48 – 47. The Foxfires had the ball, passing it among themselves to kill time. Suddenly it was intercepted!

Jerry had it, his fifth steal of the game. A resounding roar exploded from the Chariot fans as he dribbled the ball upcourt, not a single Foxfire nor Chariot near him.

"Make it yourself, Jerry!" the familiar voice of his father shouted.

He reached the basket and shot. The

ball hung on the rim a moment — then rolled off!

It seemed, as Coach Stull had said earlier, that "someone had pulled a string on it" to keep it from going in. The resounding cries died as quickly as they had started.

Two seconds later the game was over.

4

FREDDIE AND JERRY almost got into a fight in the locker room.

"You stink, Jerry," Freddie was saying. "You must be paying Coach Stull to let you play because you're next to worthless."

Jerry couldn't take it any longer and barged into Freddie, fists clenched. But Ronnie jumped between them.

"No, Jerry! No!"

An ache lodged in Jerry's throat as he looked at Ronnie, then at the glowering

face beyond. Freddie's jaw stuck out, and his fists were clenched, too.

Coach Stull stepped into the locker room. His black eyes flashed. "What's going on here?" he demanded.

"Nothing," said Ronnie. "Everything's okay now, Coach."

The coach looked at Freddie and Jerry, then at the others. "Take your showers, then get out of here. And don't put the blame for our loss on anyone. You each played an excellent game. Winning's fine, but losing is no disgrace. See you tomorrow."

Fifteen minutes later Jerry finished dressing and looked for Ronnie.

"He's gone," said Lin Foo, zipping up his jacket. "Left about five minutes ago."

Jerry headed for the door, an ache in his stomach. He didn't care if Freddie Pearse never spoke to him again, but it was different with Ronnie. Ronnie had always been a good friend, a buddy. They rode bikes together, worked for the same merit badges together, shared each other's secrets. Without Ronnie he had no one.

Oh, sure, there were Mom and Dad, but they were different. The three of them went on picnics together, to movies and to vacation spots in the mountains. But that wasn't like being with a kid your age, a kid who enjoyed doing the same things you did.

Lin Foo walked with him most of the way home, then turned off on another street. "G'night, Jerry. See you tomorrow."

"Good night, Lin."

Snow flurries whipped about like tiny white feathers, striking Jerry's cheeks and melting almost instantly. A car's headlights pierced the darkness. Jerry waited till the car passed by, then started to cross the street when somebody called his name. He paused and looked down the street. A kid was running toward him, a kid slightly shorter than he.

Jerry stepped back onto the curb and waited for him. He frowned as the figure drew closer.

"Hi, Jerry. I'm Danny Weatherspoon," the kid said. "I — I'd like to talk to you a minute."

He wore a heavy Windbreaker and was bareheaded. Jerry had never seen him before in his life.

"It's late," Jerry said. "And it's cold."

"It'll only take a minute," Danny Weatherspoon said.

Jerry shivered. "Okay, go ahead and talk."

Danny Weatherspoon looked him directly in the eyes. "Don't — don't you think it's kind of funny that you haven't been making baskets?"

Jerry blinked. What was the kid driving at?

"Well?" asked Danny.

"Yeah," Jerry replied after he was able to. "Why?"

"I'm responsible," Danny said.

Jerry stared at him. "You're *what?*"

"I'm responsible," Danny repeated. "Well — in a way, that is." Danny smiled, looked up and down the street and back again at Jerry. "The truth is, you brought this on yourself, so don't blame it all on me."

"Brought *what* on?" cried Jerry, completely baffled at what Danny Weatherspoon was trying to tell him.

"This — this *thing!*" Danny said seriously. "This — problem!"

"You're nuts," Jerry said, and started to cross the street. "Good night. I'm bushed. I've got to get some sleep."

Danny Weatherspoon hurried up alongside of him. "I'm here to help you, Jerry! Please listen, will you?"

Jerry crossed the street and stopped. "Look, Danny Weatherspoon, I don't like jokes on a cold, snowy night — especially from some kid I've never seen before. Now leave me alone, will you? Play them on somebody else. Freddie Pearse, for example. He might just *love* 'em."

"But Freddie is not a relative," Danny said.

Jerry frowned. "A relative? You mean that you're a relative of mine?"

Danny chuckled. "That's right. From

way back, and I mean way back. Three hundred years, at least."

"Mom and Dad never mentioned any Weatherspoons to me," Jerry murmured.

"Of course not. That's because they're not your natural mother and father. You do know that, don't you?"

"Sure I do. My natural parents died when I was about three."

"Right. In a car accident," said Danny.

Jerry frowned. "How did you know about that?" he asked curiously.

Danny grinned. "It's true, isn't it?"

"Well — yes." Danny's parents must have read about it in the newspaper and told him, of course. How else could he know?

Jerry saw the snow piling on Danny's head, and knew that it must be piling on his, too. He felt chilled and wanted to hurry home before he caught a cold. Mom and Dad would be wondering what had happened to him.

"What's all this got to do with my not making baskets?" he asked.

"You've been spoiling the good reputation of a Weatherspoon, and until you change for the better your shots won't get any better either," Danny said.

Jerry stared at him, and laughed. Suddenly he wasn't angry at the kid anymore. He was amused. He would play along with him for just another minute or two, then go home. It seemed that he had found a new friend, even if Danny was talking a lot of nonsense.

"What have I been doing to spoil a good reputation?" he asked.

Danny shrugged. "A lot of things, like aggravating your mother, for instance.

41

And letting your father carry out the garbage and shovel the snow when you are supposed to do those jobs yourself. And, to top it off, asking Ronnie Malone to do your book report for you. Man, that's *real* nerve!"

Jerry's heart drummed. "How — how could you know all this?" he asked huskily.

Danny's eyes twinkled. "I'm a warlock," he smiled.

"A warlock?" Jerry echoed. "What's a warlock?"

"A person with supernatural powers. A man is called a warlock, a woman is called a witch. You know what a witch is, don't you?"

"Sure I know what a witch is," Jerry replied, getting more annoyed with Danny by the minute. "Now that you've explained it to me, mind if I go home?"

"Jerry! For Petey sakes, believe me, will you? I'm serious!"

"Okay, I believe you. All right?" Anything to get rid of the obnoxious kid, whoever he was. Warlock! Oh, man!

Just then the sound of loud, screeching tires drew Jerry's attention, and he saw a red sports car cutting around the street corner at a rate of speed that must have exceeded the town's speed limit.

"Wow! Look at him go!" Jerry cried. "How would you like to have wheels like that?"

He turned to look at Danny, a fat grin on his face. Instantly the grin faded. His skin crawled.

"Danny?" he said.

But Danny seemed to have vanished. He was nowhere in sight.

5

W HAT KEPT YOU so late?" Mr.
Steele asked as Jerry pulled off his
snow-covered jacket and tossed it over the
back of a chair.

"I met a kid who said his name is
Danny Weatherspoon," Jerry replied. "He
said he's a relative of mine, and a warlock."

His father laughed. "Where does he
live?"

"Somewhere nearby. I didn't think to
ask him."

"A warlock, huh?" Mrs. Steele picked

up his jacket, shook the melting snow onto a rug near the door, and went to hang it in the closet. "What kids will do nowadays for kicks. Want something to eat, Jerry?"

"A bowl of cereal and something hot to drink," he said.

"Hot chocolate?"

"Okay."

In bed he tried to erase Danny Weatherspoon from his mind, but couldn't. How could Danny know so much about him? Danny's words echoed in his ears as he fell asleep.

The next morning he heard his mother yelling to him to get up, but he only turned over and tried to fall back to sleep. She would call again, he was sure. She always did.

Suddenly he remembered what Danny Weatherspoon had said to him, and in a flash he was out of bed, yanking on his clothes and running downstairs just as his mother was about to yell again.

She stared at him as he popped into the kitchen, panting. "I can't believe it," she exclaimed. "Is it really you, Jerry?"

He grinned. "It's really me, Mom."

He looked out of the window and saw a thick blanket of snow covering the driveway. Deep tire tracks indicated that his father had left for work without having shoveled off the snow.

"I'll shovel out the driveway before I eat, Mom," Jerry volunteered.

He put on his jacket, noticing his mother's surprised expression.

"Jerry, are you all right?" she asked.

"I'm just fine, Mom," he smiled.

He got the shovel from the garage and had the driveway half shoveled out when

his mother yelled to him from a window, "You don't have to shovel it all now, Jerry! Leave the rest of it for this afternoon!"

A good idea, he thought. He was getting tired, anyway, and it wasn't absolutely necessary that he finish it now. His father wouldn't be home till about 5:30, by which time Jerry, starting after school, could have the driveway shoveled out clean. He put the shovel away and went into the house.

He took a shower, then sat down for breakfast, feeling hungry enough to eat a whole hog. Well, two eggs and two slices of toast, anyway, which were what his mother made for him.

That afternoon, when he returned home from school, he finished shoveling off the driveway. When Mr. Steele drove in his expression clearly indicated that he couldn't believe what he saw.

"Who did you hire to do that?" he asked Mrs. Steele.

She smiled and nodded at Jerry. "Your son did it."

Mr. Steele's eyes brightened. "Good work, son. I had a rough day, and thinking about shoveling off this driveway when I got home made it rougher. Thanks very much."

Jerry didn't tell him that he had done it just to see if being obedient and cooperative at home could have anything to do with his making baskets. What nonsense! How could it possibly have a connection? A guy has to be a nut to believe such garbage.

Nonetheless, he decided he would go

one step farther. After supper he would wash and dry the dishes. If Mom and Dad wondered if there were an ulterior motive in his being such an eager beaver all of a sudden, he would think of an explanation.

"Jerry! What do you think you're doing?" his mother asked as he cleared the table after supper and started to run water into a large pan in the sink.

"You and Dad sit in the living room and relax, Mom," Jerry said. "I'll do the dishes."

"I can't believe it!" she cried. "What's got into you?"

"Nothing. I just want to give you and Dad a day off. Isn't that all right?"

She looked at him a long moment before she answered. "Yes, of course, it is, and we appreciate it a lot. But you don't have to overdo it, you know. We don't want you to get so tired that you won't want to do it again. Let me wash the dishes and you dry them."

Well, I won't argue with her, Jerry thought. So she washed and he dried.

On Thursday night, December 9, the Chariots played the Peacocks. The game started with Jerry on the bench. He couldn't believe it. Even as he watched the short, stocky player running out there, catching a pass, throwing it, jumping for a rebound and not getting anywhere near it, Jerry couldn't believe that Coach Stull would start Manny Lucas instead of him.

Immediately he thought of the chores he had done at home — the hard work of shoveling off the driveway and the easy job of drying the supper dishes — and he told himself that he had wasted his time. Believing a single word that Danny

51

Weatherspoon had told him was like believing in elves and leprechauns.

He looked around for Danny and saw him sitting among a group of guys on the top row. Danny waved and Jerry waved back, though not enthusiastically. Frankly, he was hoping that Danny had stayed away.

Freddie Pearse sank the first basket for the Chariots, then Ronnie was fouled and managed to sink one out of two. The Peacock playing opposite Manny was fast and handled the ball well, scoring twice and even stealing the ball once from the stocky Chariot. Jerry covered his eyes and wondered how long Coach Stull would keep Manny in there.

The Peacocks crept up to a 13 – 8 lead. Then — Jerry could hardly believe his eyes — Manny sank a twenty-footer! The Chariot fans roared and Manny grinned, taking a bow as he ran upcourt.

Jerry couldn't help but smile, too. Manny deserved a basket once in a while.

But so do I, Jerry thought. *Why can't I sink one? And now, while I'm warming the bench, what chance have I got to get back into the groove again? How long will the coach have me sit here?*

There were two minutes left in the first quarter when Coach Stull sent Jerry in to replace Manny. Jerry, caught by surprise, wasn't ready. He had practically accepted the fact that he wouldn't be playing at all the first quarter.

After reporting to the scorekeeper he ran in and met Freddie Pearse's eyes squarely.

"I was wishing you'd sit out this whole game," Freddie said evenly. "Manny was doing fine."

"I knew you'd be happy to see me come in," Jerry replied.

Freddie glowered at him and looked away, shaking his head. Jerry knew he had to play harder now, harder than he had ever played before, to keep the team together and to show Freddie a thing or two.

6

JERRY GOT THE BALL only once during those two minutes. Even though he was in the open several times no one passed to him. Not until he ran to a corner on a hard press by the Peacocks did Ronnie pass him the ball.

"Shoot!" a voice Jerry recognized as Danny's shouted. "Shoot, Jerry!"

Nervously Jerry stood looking at the basket, the ball gripped in his hands. He wanted to shoot, but he was afraid he would miss. He had missed so many times before.

"Jerry, shoot!"

Jerry never saw the Peacock sweeping in until the player hit the ball out of his hands. He hustled to retrieve it. But the Peacock, a little dynamo, dribbled it away and passed it downcourt to a teammate. Seconds later the Peacocks scored another basket. 15 – 10.

Jerry ran downcourt in a daze. He felt that every eye in the gym was on him. He bumped into Chuck Metz, who almost tripped over his own feet as he tried to regain his balance.

"Look where you're going, will you?" Chuck snorted.

"Sorry," Jerry murmured.

The first quarter ended, and Coach Stull rose from the bench as the guys crowded around him. "You seem to be in a fog out there, Jerry," he said. "You all right?"

Jerry nodded.

"I don't think he is, Coach," Chuck said. "Did you see him run into me?"

Jerry glared at him, looked at the coach, then at the floor.

"Something's really bothering him, Coach," Freddie said. "He doesn't know what he's doing out there."

"Nothing's bothering me," Jerry grunted, trying to keep his temper under control. "You guys were freezing me out. What do you expect me to do?"

"You haven't scored a point this year," Freddie snapped. "What do you expect *us* to do?"

"All right, cut it out," Coach Stull ordered. "We can't have a team of squabblers. I want you to start the second quarter, Jerry. If you need warming up you'll have the chance. Okay, get together out there and play basketball like you mean it. We're trailing 15 – 10. Let's get in front for a change."

It took Jerry a minute for the sweat to start shining on his face and shoulders. He ran and passed and found several good opportunities to shoot. Instead, though, he passed to Ronnie, Chuck or Freddie, while Lin Foo guarded the back court.

Ronnie sank two, one a lay-up, the other from a corner. Chuck plunked in a basket from the foul line, and Freddie laid up two, drawing a foul shot on one of them and making it. But the Peacocks didn't give up. They dropped three baskets through the net and scored two foul shots. The half ended. Peacocks 23, Chariots 21.

Jerry headed for the locker room for a thirst-quenching slice of orange, and rest. "Jerry, wait!" a voice called, and he saw Danny Weatherspoon come running up beside him.

"Why aren't you shooting, Jerry?" Danny asked anxiously. "You're passing up a lot of good shots."

"Why do you think I'm not shooting?" Jerry said. "I've got a hundred zeros chalked up after my name already."

He had started to walk through the doorway leading down to the locker room, when Danny stopped him. "Jerry, wait a minute. I want to talk to you."

Jerry paused and looked at him. "I'm sorry, Danny, but I haven't got time now. I'm beat and thirsty. Besides, Coach Stull will want to talk to us. I'll see you after the game. Okay?"

Danny looked disappointed. "It'll be too late then."

"Too late for what?"

Just then, someone grabbed Jerry's arm and pulled him toward the door. "Come on, Jerry. Time's a-wastin'."

Jerry looked up at the coach's face as he let himself be led through the doorway. He grinned nervously, then looked back at Danny. "See you later, Danny!" he cried.

Danny nodded, looking glum and unhappy. *Poor kid,* Jerry thought. *He feels as bad about my not making baskets as I do.*

The Peacocks bolstered their lead by six points in the third quarter before Freddie dumped in a long one, the Chariots' first score in the second half. Jerry, jumping like an uncoiling spring, intercepted

the bounce from out-of-bounds and dribbled the ball upcourt before the Peacocks knew what had happened. He was double-teamed in an instant and brought himself up short, faking a pass over and under the Peacocks' heads as he kept pivoting on one foot.

"Shoot, Jerry!" Danny's voice rose above the din.

Jerry looked for someone to pass to. But Ronnie, Chuck, Freddie and even Lin Foo were all covered.

Jerry leaped, lifting the ball up over his head with both hands, then shot. The ball arced toward the hoop, dropped and slithered through the net!

A crashing roar exploded from the Chariot fans. "Great shot, Jerry!" his father's voice boomed.

"That-a-boy, Jerry! *That-a-boy!*" Danny

Weatherspoon's voice almost cracked as he yelled.

Jerry could hardly believe it. His first basket! He had sunk his first basket!

"Just because you made that shot," Freddie growled, "don't think you've suddenly gotten lucky."

"Lucky or not, I feel lots better," Jerry replied, smiling. "I've cracked the ice."

Both teams racked up more points before the quarter ended, but Jerry didn't have a chance for another shot until the start of the last quarter. Now, taking a set shot from a corner, he watched the big orange sphere drop through the hoop — again without touching the rim!

"Guess I was lucky again," he grinned at Freddie.

Freddie shrugged and ran back up the court.

The Chariots crept up on the Peacocks, and called time when there was still a minute to play. They were trailing, 51 – 48. Coach Stull talked to his boys, urging them not to let the three-point deficit discourage them.

"It's our ball," the coach told them. "Play it safe, and make your passes good. But don't waste time. That minute will go by very fast. Okay. Get in there and fight."

Jerry took out the ball. He passed it to Ronnie, who passed it back to Jerry as he raced upcourt. Jerry dribbled up the middle, then cut sharply toward the sideline, pursued by his man. He stopped, pivoted, and looked for a man to pass to. The Peacocks had every Chariot covered.

Then Freddie pulled away from his guard and Jerry passed to him. The Peacock guard jumped in front of Freddie, struck the ball and again Jerry got it. He was near the basket this time, but it was behind him. He leaped, twisted, and shot. As he did, a Peacock struck his arm and the whistle shrilled.

7

THE BALL HIT THE BACKBOARD and went in. Jerry stared at the ref, wondering if the score counted. It did!

Then he saw the ref raise a finger. "One shot!" the ref yelled, and pointed at the offender. The Peacock lifted his arm and turned away sheepishly.

"You'll make it, Jerry!" Danny yelled.

Jerry caught the toss from the ref, stood at the foul line, bounced the ball a few times, then shot. The ball arced neatly and dropped in. Peacocks 51, Chariots 51.

Jerry looked at the time remaining as he

rushed to cover the man taking the ball out-of-bounds. Thirty seconds to go.

The Peacock passed the ball by him and Jerry turned and rushed after the receiver. Two quick passes and the Peacocks had the ball at their end of the court. They played cautiously now, letting the seconds tick away while they waited for the right moment to shoot.

"Get that ball!" Coach Stull shouted. "Get that ball!"

Even before the coach had yelled the second time, Jerry was sprinting after the ball handler. He swept in from behind, struck the ball out of the Peacock's hand, grabbed it and dribbled it away.

He was double-teamed instantly. But up ahead, running toward his basket, was Ronnie Malone. Jerry heaved the ball to him, throwing it ahead of the tall forward

so that Ronnie could catch it on the run. The throw was perfect. Ronnie caught it, stopped, turned and shot. A hit!

Seconds later the buzzer sounded. The game was over. Peacocks 51, Chariots 53.

There was rejoicing, a lot of backslapping, and hand shaking.

"I suppose I ought to say I'm sorry," Freddie said as he walked with Jerry to the locker room.

"Forget it," replied Jerry.

"I'll say it before I do," Freddie said. "I'm sorry."

Jerry grinned. "Okay. Thanks. But maybe I am just lucky."

After he showered and dressed, Jerry walked out of the building and found Danny Weatherspoon waiting for him. The little guy was smiling happily.

"Nice game, Jerry," he said.

"Thanks, Danny. You didn't stick around just to tell me that, though, did you? It's late."

"I know," Danny said. "But I just had to tell you how pleased I am."

"Okay, you're pleased. But don't give me any bull that you had something to do with it," Jerry said seriously. "You're not going to make me believe *that*."

Danny shrugged. "Believe what you want to, but you did score a few points tonight, the first time this season."

"Sure. But that's because I've been due."

Danny smiled. "Okay, Jerry. Have it your way. But do me a favor, will you?"

"If I can, sure. Why not?"

"Don't disappoint your parents again. They were very happy that you helped out with some of their hard work at home."

Jerry sighed. This kid was too much. "Okay, Danny. Anything you say. After all, who am I to disappoint a relative?"

They headed down the street, their steps a crunching sound on the snow-crusted sidewalk. Suddenly, Jerry stopped. "Hey, Danny, if you're a warlock like you say, and we're distantly related, doesn't that make me a —"

"Afraid not," Danny interrupted. "In some branches of the family, the strain of magic in the Weatherspoons died out. I'm afraid that was true of your father. That's why it's all the more important that we warlock Weatherspoons take an interest in you unlucky ones!"

Jerry raised his eyebrows but didn't say

71

anything as he pulled the collar of his jacket up to cover his ears against the bone-chilling air.

"You know, if you'd really like to do something for me — something *else* for me — get Freddie Pearse off my back," he suggested, not being able to think of anything else to say to break the silence.

"Impossible," replied Danny. "We have nothing in common."

Jerry frowned at him. "You mean you can't put the zap on him?"

"That's right."

"Why not?"

"He's not a relative."

"Oh, I see."

"I wish I could, though," Danny confessed. "I've noticed how he torments you. He has a very cruel nature at times. Frankly, I'm glad he isn't a relative."

"So am I," grunted Jerry.

They arrived at the intersection where their paths separated, said good night to each other, and went on their ways.

What a kid, Jerry thought as he looked up at the star-studded sky. *He really believes he's a warlock!*

But something that Danny had said suddenly came back to him. *Believe what you want to, but you did score a few points tonight, the first time this season.* Was it coincidence, or did Danny really have something to do with it?

Well, there was a way to find out, beginning tomorrow morning.

8

"JERRY! TIME to get up!"

He awakened promptly at the sound of his mother's voice, looked at the sunshine coming through the window, then turned over and waited to sink into the sweet bliss of sleep again. Those few extra winks always felt so good, and he didn't have to worry about being late for school. Mom would be yelling again, that's for sure.

"Jerry! Up an' at 'em, son! Come on!"

He awoke from a wild dream — he had been on a sailboat bucking high waves,

74

and Freddie Pearse was manning the tiller. Jerry found himself still rocking as he opened his eyes. He stared at the face smiling down at him. Then the rocking stopped and he saw that the face belonged to his mother.

"Man, what a wild dream I had!" he said, rubbing his eyes.

"I had to shake you awake," his mother said. "You were sleeping very soundly."

"I heard you the first time, Mom," he confessed. "But I fell back to sleep."

"Oh? Are you back in the old rut again?"

The remark stung a little. "Oh, Mom, you don't have to put it that way," he said.

She patted him on the cheek and left. He got up, dressed and went downstairs.

"Look out of the window," his mother said.

He did, and saw the driveway covered

with a new blanket of snow. Twin tracks showed where his father had driven out earlier to go to work.

Jerry felt guilty for not having gotten up the first time his mother had called him. He would've had time to shovel out a part of the driveway, at least. On the other hand, he was glad that he had stayed in bed. For one thing, shoveling snow was no picnic. For another thing, he was going to prove that Danny Weatherspoon was no warlock.

"Mom, do you believe in warlocks?" he asked as he sat down for breakfast.

"Now, Jerry," she said, smiling at him from across the table. "Are you serious? Warlocks were believed to exist in witchcraft days, but that was purely superstition." She paused. "Are you thinking of Danny Weatherspoon again?"

He shrugged. "Yeah," he admitted.

"Why don't you invite him here some-time? I'd like to meet him."

"Okay."

If he's a warlock he won't come, thought Jerry. *He won't know how to behave in front of non-warlock parents!*

That afternoon, when Jerry saw Danny and invited him to his home, Danny expressed complete delight. Jerry's jaw fell open. He couldn't believe it.

"You mean you don't mind?"

"Of course, I don't mind!" said Danny, his eyes sparkling. "Why should I?"

Jerry shook his head. "Yeah. Why should you? Want to come over for supper?"

"I'd be happy to. But first, you'd better ask your mother if it's okay."

"Oh, it's okay, all right. I'm sure of it."

Then he stared at Danny. "How do you know I haven't asked her already?"

Danny grinned that elfish grin of his. "Ask her, will you, please?"

"Okay. I'll ask her."

When Jerry arrived home, he asked his mother if it was okay for Danny to come for supper, and she said of course it was. He started to the phone to call up Danny and suddenly realized that he didn't know Danny's number. Not only that, he didn't even know where Danny lived.

He looked in the phone directory for Danny's number, but there was no Weatherspoon listed.

He put on his coat and walked out of the house, hoping that he would run across the little guy. He did — just as he reached the corner of the street. Danny was bundled up in a heavy coat and hood.

"Hi!" Jerry cried. "You're just the guy I'm looking for!"

"About the supper?" Danny asked.

"Right," said Jerry. "Mom says it's okay."

"Fine. Want me to come now?"

"Why not?"

They went to Jerry's house and Jerry introduced Danny to his mother. Then he took Danny to his room and showed him his antique model cars. They were lined up diagonally in neat rows on three shelves, ten on each shelf.

"What a beautiful collection!" Danny exclaimed. "Did you assemble them yourself?"

"Of course," Jerry said proudly.

"Every single bit of them?"

"Every single bit."

"Hmm," murmured Danny.

"Okay. So my father helped me," Jerry confessed. "But I did *most* of the work."

Danny smiled. He looked at the pictures on one of the walls, pictures of racing cars from the earliest days of racing down to the present. On another wall were basketball pictures cut out from magazines, and autographed photos of basketball players. Danny looked impressed.

He pulled open a drawer. "Wow!" he cried, and stared at Jerry.

Jerry slammed the drawer shut. "What're you looking at me like that for?" he said tightly.

"That's an awful lot of pens," Danny said. "And most of them have somebody else's name on 'em."

Jerry's heart pounded. "They're cheap pens. Nobody missed them."

"So what? You've got to give them back, Jerry."

Jerry tried to hide his embarrassment and control his temper at the same time. Danny had no business opening that drawer. That was going too far.

"Are you going to tell people that I took their pens?" he asked.

"No."

The silence that followed hung over them like a heavy sheet. Jerry could hear his mother's footsteps on the kitchen floor, and dishes scraping as she set the table.

"Why, Jerry?" Danny asked imploringly. "Why did you take them?"

Jerry shrugged. "I was always losing my own, that's why. Then one day Dad told me I'd better not lose another one because he wasn't going to buy me any more pens."

"So you started to gather up a collection from the kids in school."

Jerry nodded. "I know it's not right, but —"

"Not right?" Danny stared at him. "Jerry! That's stealing! You might get in real trouble!"

"I know." Jerry paused. "Okay. I'll give them back — every single one of them."

His mother's yell for them to come to supper interrupted further discussion about the pens. Mr. Steele had come home and Jerry introduced Danny to him, adding that he was a new friend who lived a few blocks away.

"Got any hobbies, Danny?" Mrs. Steele asked after they began to eat.

"Oh, yes," replied Danny. "Several."

"What's your favorite?"

"Reading."

"What kind of reading?"

"Old American history."

"Oh? That's very interesting."

Jerry saw a twinkle in his mother's eyes, and his pulse quickened. Did she think she had trapped Danny? Was Danny's answer conclusive evidence that his story about being a warlock was due to his reading so much on old American history?

"As a matter of fact," Danny went on to say, "I think that the seventeenth century was more fascinating than any other time in our history."

"Is that so?" Mr. Steele's eyebrows arched with interest. "Why's that, Danny?"

Danny chewed on a hunk of food before answering. "Because it was a period when many people believed in witchcraft," he said. "And a lot of innocent people died through no fault of their own. It was a horrible time to live."

"That's right, Danny. It sure was," agreed Mr. Steele.

Jerry's heart skipped a beat as he looked from his father to his mother, noticing the warm smile they exchanged with each other.

He was glad when supper was over and he and Danny could leave the table. He was hoping that Danny would want to go home so that there would not be any more discussion about witchcraft. But Danny seemed to be in no hurry to leave. As a matter of fact, Danny said, "Come on, Jerry. Let's help your mother do the dishes."

9

"IS OLD AMERICAN HISTORY really your favorite kind of reading?" Jerry asked as he and Danny, bundled in their warm clothes, walked down the street together.

"Of course it is. Why?"

Jerry shrugged. "It's just peculiar, that's all. Most kids like anything else *but* old — or even new — American history. Mom and Dad didn't embarrass you with their questions, did they?"

"Don't be silly. As a matter of fact, I anticipated their questions." Danny's eyes twinkled. "I've been through that before, Jerry."

They reached the end of the third block when Danny said, "We're halfway to my home, Jerry. Thanks for walking this far with me, and for inviting me for supper."

"That's okay," said Jerry. "Good night, Danny."

"Good night, Jerry."

When Jerry arrived home he took off his coat and found his mother and father relaxing in the living room. His father was sitting on his favorite lounge chair, reading the evening paper, and his mother was mending a shirt.

"Well, what do you think of him?" Jerry asked.

"Of Danny?" His mother smiled. "He's a very nice boy. Smart, too, and well-mannered."

"You've found a nice friend," his father said. "Don't lose him."

"Now you know where he gets his ideas about warlocks," his mother added.

"Yes," Jerry replied. "From reading old American history."

Jerry didn't see Danny during the next two days, but thought nothing of it. Everyone was staying indoors as much as they could since the temperature had dropped to a few degrees below zero.

More days went by and Jerry still didn't see Danny. One sunny, not-too-cold day he walked near the neighborhood where he first saw Danny but saw him nowhere. Now and then Ronnie Malone stopped in to visit Jerry and Jerry visited him. They were still the best of friends. But not seeing Danny Weatherspoon all this time began to leave a void in Jerry's life. What had happened to the little guy, anyway?

Meanwhile Jerry got back into his regular routine again. It was so easy for him not to take his mother seriously whenever she ordered him to do things, like getting rid of the cobwebs in the basement. What was wrong with cobwebs? Who saw them, anyway? And weren't spiders beneficial? They trapped flies and moths in their webs and ate them up, didn't they?

The garbage was a problem, too. Jerry had promised his mother that he would carry it out at night for sure. But when the time came he would neglect to do so, and his father would have to carry it out before he left for work in the morning.

And his dirty clothes. His mother wanted him to put on clean clothes every day and to take his dirty ones down to the laundry room every morning. But he seldom did. *Why carry them down every day,* he reasoned, *when Mom launders only a couple of times a week anyway? She can pick them up when she cleans the room. Why all the fuss about cleanliness, anyway?*

"Ronnie," Jerry asked his friend one day, "do your parents make you do a lot of chores around the house?"

"Well, I mow the lawn."

"In winter?"

"No. In summer, lunkhead."

"What do you do in winter?"

"I always carry out the garbage — in winter and summer," Ronnie replied. "And every time the bottles pile up, I take them to the special bin out in back of the grocery store. Most of them are being recycled."

"Your parents pay you for doing all that?"

"Heck, no. Why should they pay me?"

Jerry looked at him a long minute. "Forget it," he said.

The Chariots had intrasquad practice on Tuesday, December 14, and Jerry started. He looked for Danny among the few scattered fans sitting in the bleachers, but didn't see him.

"Ronnie, have you seen Danny Weatherspoon lately?" he asked.

"Danny who?"

"Danny Weatherspoon. A little guy. Has dark hair, wears a heavy coat."

"Is that so? A little guy, has dark hair and wears a heavy coat. Do you know

91

how many guys go to our school who look like that?"

Jerry stared. "You don't know Danny?"

"No, I don't know Danny."

Freddie Pearse walked up to Jerry and looked him straight in his eyes. "Jerry, if you want to yak, sit on the bench. You do a lot better job yakking than playing, anyway."

"You must've forgotten who sparked the team in that last game, Freddie," Jerry said, standing up to Freddie without twitching a muscle.

"If you ask me, you were just lucky," Freddie said.

"I'm not asking you," said Jerry.

The whistle shrilled and Coach Stull yelled, "C'mon, you guys! Let's get the show moving!"

Freddie gave Jerry a burning look before he turned and walked to his center position. Opposite him was the team's alternate center, Pat Wilson, who was as tall as Freddie but who lacked the spring in his jump that Freddie had. Freddie outjumped him, tapping the ball to Chuck Metz, who dribbled quickly upcourt, then passed to Lin Foo. Lin dribbled up closer to the basket, then almost fell as a couple of opponents swarmed over him. He passed to Jerry and Jerry took a shot. The throw looked perfect. The ball struck the boards and bounced into —

No, it didn't! It hit the rim and bounced off!

"Tough luck, Jerry!" Ronnie cried.

Freddie caught the rebound and laid it up. The ball dropped smoothly through the net, and Freddie, running downcourt, glared at Jerry.

"Just pass the ball, Jerry," he said. "If you keep on shooting we're going to freeze you out."

Jerry stared at him. "Freeze me out? That shot just missed by a hair!"

"A miss is as good as a mile," Freddie grunted.

Once, later on, Jerry had another chance to shoot, and took it. He was in the clear and all of his teammates were thoroughly covered. The ball struck the rim, bounced halfway to the ceiling, then dropped. It headed directly for the middle of the hoop — but suddenly, as if a string had pulled it, it struck the rim and bounced off.

"Oh, no!" Jerry moaned.

"Number two!" Freddie yelled. "Okay, Jerry! You asked for it!"

Jerry was too disheartened to run in for

the rebound. Pat Wilson caught it, took it upcourt and shot a long pass to a teammate waiting near his basket. The kid caught the ball and laid it up for an easy two points.

The whistle shrilled and Jerry saw Freddie walking over to the coach. Freddie said something, then both he and Coach Stull looked at Jerry.

The rat! Jerry thought. *Freddie's probably told the coach to take me out!*

The coach said something to Freddie, and Freddie came trotting back onto the court, his face cherry red.

"What's up, Freddie?" Chuck Metz asked.

"Nothing," Freddie said.

I bet, Jerry thought. *"Nothing," the way Freddie had said it, meant "a lot."*

The scrimmage continued, but Jerry

96

lacked the spirit and the energy that he had earlier. Knowing that Freddie Pearse was angry because Coach Stull was permitting Jerry to stay in the game sapped the strength out of him. Jerry didn't shoot after that, nor did the guys pass to him as often as they had. They were already beginning the freeze.

As the freeze continued, Jerry noticed the change in the first team's play. Both Lin Foo and Chuck Metz, although fast runners, weren't good dribblers. Twice the ball was stolen from them, each time resulting in a basket for the second team. Also, by freezing out Jerry, their pass patterns went awry. The team was disorganized. Only because the second team was inferior in every respect was the first team able to outplay them.

In the locker room after the game Jerry

overheard Ronnie say to Freddie, "I don't like the idea of freezing Jerry out. I think it's mean."

"Why? Because he's your friend?"

"Because he's my friend and because it's mean, that's why."

"What good is a guy if he shoots and never hits?" Freddie snapped.

"Jerry's the best dribbler we've got," Ronnie countered. "And he's good on the rebounds. Even better than you are, and he's shorter."

"My eye," said Freddie.

Jerry smiled to himself. Nobody but a real friend would stick up for him as Ronnie had.

He showered, dressed, and found Ronnie waiting for him near the door.

"Thanks for speaking up for me," Jerry said as they left the warm smell of the locker room behind them and stepped out into the chill night air.

"He had it coming," Ronnie said.

They waited for a car to pass by, then crossed the street.

"When's our next game?" Jerry asked.

"Thursday," said Ronnie. "It's another scrimmage. We don't play a league game again until next Tuesday against the Skylarks."

Jerry was silent a moment. "I won't be there," he said finally.

Ronnie frowned. "Why not?"

"I'm going to be sick that night," Jerry replied.

10

JERRY KEPT HIS PROMISE. He didn't show up for the game.

He started to read a book on antique and classic cars, but couldn't concentrate on it. He knew that his place was at the game, not here. Even though it was a scrimmage, even though he might not make a single basket, he should have gone to the game.

Darn it! he thought. *It's all Freddie Pearse's fault!*

Freddie was the real reason why Jerry didn't go. Sometimes Chuck Metz and the other guys made remarks to Jerry about his missing shots, but it was Freddie who really was the dirty one.

He's the one who climbs all over my back whenever I miss, Jerry thought despairingly. *He never considers how hard I play. He overlooks the times when I steal the ball from an opponent, pick off rebounds, and dribble the ball upcourt to make it possible for him and the other guys to shoot. No, he thinks that I should make baskets, too.*

Jerry was quiet at the breakfast table the next morning.

"Jerry, I haven't heard you say a word about Danny Weatherspoon lately," his mother said.

"I haven't seen him," Jerry said.

"Oh? Do you suppose he isn't well?"

"I don't know."

101

At about 10:00 Jerry was in the school corridor, heading for math class, when someone poked him on the shoulder. He turned, and couldn't believe his eyes.

"Danny!" he cried, and looked at the red bell-bottom pants and blue shirt Danny wore. "Man, do you look sharp!"

Danny grinned. "Thanks, Jerry. My mother thinks I should wear clothes according to the custom of the times."

"Yeah, you sure look better," Jerry agreed. "Where have you been during the last week?"

"Home. And here. Oh, I know what *you've* been doing. That's what I want to see you about."

Jerry frowned. "Now? This minute?"

"This minute," Danny said. "Come on. Let's get out of this traffic."

He elbowed Jerry around the corner of the hall. "Jerry, you'll have to get on the ball," he said emphatically. "You haven't paid the slightest attention to what I've been telling you."

"About my doing things at home, you mean?"

"Not things, Jerry! Duties! Your behavior is a disgrace to you and the Weatherspoons! Of all the relatives in our warlock ancestry you are just about the most — well, I can't describe it."

"Then don't try," said Jerry.

"Can't you understand that I'm trying to help you for your own good?" Danny persisted. "Unless you mend your ways you'll continue through life just the way you have been on the basketball court. Basketball is only one of the many ways in which you can suffer for your shameful behavior. Am I getting through to you, Jerry?"

"You're all wet, Danny," Jerry said seriously. "I'm not going to be a goody-goody to satisfy you or any other 'warlock ancestor' of mine. You're wasting your time."

"I'm not asking you to be a goody-goody. Nor an angel, either. I'm just asking you to live decently, not to steal, and to love your parents by showing it. Is anything wrong with that?"

Jerry admitted there wasn't.

"Then will you please get off your high horse and start working at it?" Danny said. "You come from a distinguished family, Jerry. You're different from other people." Danny smiled. "Really, it's no disgrace being related to warlocks. It's a lot of fun most of the time. Who knows?

Maybe some day *you* may be asked to help a warlock relative yourself!"

"Don't count on it," muttered Jerry.

A buzzer rang.

"See you at the next game, Jerry," Danny said. "And please be there." He left.

"Warlocks," Jerry mumbled as he headed for his classroom. "I still don't know whether to believe that baloney or not. I don't *feel* related to a warlock. Isn't it supposed to make you feel differently?"

Jerry ignored Danny's advice. Oh, he wasn't going to do anything wild or far out to purposely prove that what Danny said was hogwash; he was just going to live his life normally, that's all. Any other way would mean that he was taking Danny seriously. And he wouldn't do that for all the nickels in the world.

"A warlock!" Jerry said again, disgustedly. "What does he take me for? A nut?"

There were several incidents that came up before the next game that gave Jerry an opportunity to prove that Danny was just a fraud. He didn't get up in the morning when his mother first called him, and he *borrowed* a bright blue felt-tipped pen from a girl's desk with no intention of returning it. He took it for three reasons: one, he liked its looks; two, he didn't have one himself; and three, the girl could always buy another one.

He also tore two pictures out of a library book on antique and classic cars to add to his collection, telling himself that nobody would miss them. See if warlock Danny Weatherspoon would find out about *that!*

He thought of excuses to avoid helping

his mother do the supper dishes, lied that he had a headache when she asked him to go to the store, and spent two hours at Ronnie's house one evening, coming home too late to write an essay on pollution which had to be turned in the next day.

Although he knew that every one of those deeds was a violation of what Danny called decent living, Jerry didn't think that any of them would hurt anybody. He, himself, felt guilty about them — but not too guilty. He was just following the whims of his nature, he told himself, hoping that his excuse was logical.

He could hardly wait for the next game. It was on Tuesday, December 21, against the Skylarks. He hadn't touched a basketball since last Tuesday when the Chariots had played an intrasquad game.

A large crowd filled the bleachers, including Jerry's mother and father. While warming up before the game Jerry looked for and saw Danny Weatherspoon on the top row of the bleachers. He tried to catch Danny's attention, but the little guy was busy talking with the boy beside him.

At last the referee blew his whistle, announcing the start of the game. But Jerry didn't start. Manny Lucas played in his place.

The Skylarks' tall, dark-haired center, Stretch Peters, outjumped Freddie, and in no time the ball was at the Skylarks' end of the court. Quick passes, evasive action, and a hook shot resulted in the Skylarks drawing first blood.

Manny took the ball out-of-bounds, tossed it in to Ronnie, and the forward moved the ball upcourt. He passed to Freddie, who tried a long shot and missed. Freddie ran in, nabbed the rebound and went up with it. This time the ball dropped through the net.

The Skylarks scored again, and drew a one-shot foul as Manny recklessly charged a Skylark taking the lay-up shot that went in. The three points put the Skylarks in front, 5 – 2.

They gained nine more within the next five minutes against the Chariots' four, and five of those were sunk by Manny's man.

"Take Manny's place, Jerry," Coach Stull said. "Stop that Skylark or he'll sink us alone."

Jerry reported to the scorekeeper, then went in when the Chariots called time. "Sorry, Manny," Jerry said.

"Oh, not you again," said Freddie. "What does Coach Stull expect you to do? Fire us up?"

"He wants me to stop that Skylark from getting more baskets," Jerry said softly.

"Isn't that nice? That Skylark's name is Jeff Sanders and he's one of the highest scorers in the league. And you expect to stop him?"

"I'm going to try," Jerry promised.

"That's all you will do — try," Freddie said, and wiped his sweat-beaded forehead.

Time-in was called and Lin Foo took the ball out for the Chariots. Jerry caught the throw-in and started to peg the ball to Ronnie. A Skylark vaulted in front of him, intercepted the throw and heaved it to a teammate downcourt.

Jerry stared, hardly believing it. That

had *never* happened to him before.

"Nice play, Jerry!" Freddie yelled. "You sure could stop anybody playing like that!"

11

J ERRY TURNED OUT to be as ineffective against the Skylark forward as Manny was. He was almost worse. Once he accidentally tripped the player and the ref called it a foul. The Skylark sank the shot. At another time Jerry bolted in to stop the player from taking a set shot, and slipped and knocked him down, a violation that gave the Skylark two shots. Fortunately the Skylark sank only one.

Lin Foo scored a lay-up and sank a foul shot to make the score 21 – 11 in the Skylarks' favor when the first quarter ended.

"Coach," Freddie's voice was loud and brittle as he looked at the coach during intermission, "are you going to keep Jerry —" He faltered. "Sorry. Forget it."

Jerry blushed. Nothing ever pleased Freddie more than having a scapegoat to blame for the team's not doing well. Especially a scapegoat whom he had never liked in the first place. Jerry understood the reason why perfectly.

About a year ago, during basketball season, Jerry had been dropping in baskets from all over the front court with a regularity that earned him the honor of being best player of the year. Second highest in scoring was Freddie. Jerry was certain that it was because he beat out Freddie that Freddie held a grudge.

Coach Stull looked at Jerry. "Kid, for some reason or other you're way off target.

You're not playing half as well as you played last year and I'm at a loss to understand why. Is something bothering you?"

Jerry shook his head. "No. Nothing's bothering me."

Danny Weatherspoon came to his mind, but he couldn't mention Danny. If he said that Danny was a warlock, they'd laugh him off the court. Jerry was really inclined to believe now that his playing was once again so poor that what Danny said could be true — he was a warlock.

"Maybe you'll snap out of it eventually," Coach Stull said. "In the meantime, I think you'd better rest a while."

Feeling everyone's eyes on him, Jerry looked at the floor and said nothing. As soon as the horn blew to start the second quarter, he left the circle of men and sat down.

The Skylarks had control of the ball during most of the quarter and led 31 – 19 when the half ended.

It wasn't until the fourth quarter that the coach had him go in again. The Skylarks now led 44 – 29, a lead that almost assured them of a win.

Jerry saw the dirty look that Freddie Pearse shot at him, and wished that the coach had kept him on the bench. The thrill of the game had been drained out of him. He lacked not only the enthusiasm to play, but also the strength. All he would do is make himself more humiliated.

A minute went by and he didn't get the ball once. It was obvious that the guys were freezing him out, and he couldn't blame them. Anybody could see that he was practically worthless.

He saw Danny in the stands. For a moment their eyes met, and Danny shook his head sadly from side to side.

Jerry wanted help from him, but was sure he wouldn't get it. Danny wasn't one to go back on his word. At least not under these conditions. Whatever Jerry wanted, he had to earn.

Jerry was alone in a corner on the front court when Ronnie dribbled the ball across the keyhole and snapped a pass to him. Caught by surprise by the unexpected throw, Jerry almost missed it. He clamped his hands tightly on the ball, glanced around for someone to pass to, and saw Freddie's hands fluttering high in the air. But Freddie's guard was on him like a leech, and Jerry was afraid that a pass to the Chariot center might be intercepted.

"Shoot, Jerry! Shoot!" the coach yelled.

Jerry shot. The ball arced through the air and headed directly for the center of the hoop. It struck the side of the rim and bounced off.

Jerry, running forward the instant he had shot, caught the rebound and tossed it to Ronnie. Ronnie rose out of the cluster of players and laid the ball up and into the net for two points.

In the din of voices Jerry picked out one he recognized. It was his father's. "Nice play, Jerry!"

During the next few seconds as the ref took the ball to the sideline to hand over to a Skylark, Jerry looked up into the sea of faces. His mother was at home recovering from the flu, but he saw his father, and felt his chest tighten.

They've been so good to me, he thought, *and I've just taken them for granted. After this game is over I'll start making it up to them. Just wait and see.*

The remaining minutes seemed endless. Jerry had to sit the last two out, which he didn't mind. He had decided that after this game was over he would turn over a new leaf. He would never steal again, and he would show his parents how much he really loved them.

The Skylarks won, 58 – 43, and Jerry rushed to the locker room to be among the first to shower and get out of the place. There was a kid he wanted to see, a kid who would also be waiting to see him.

Quickly he showered, dressed, and hurried outside. But the street was empty. Danny Weatherspoon was nowhere in sight.

12

THE NEXT MORNING Jerry rose at the first sound of his mother's voice, washed and dressed, then tried fixing his bed. He did the best he could and went downstairs, taking the clothes he had worn yesterday with him.

"Good morning, Mom," he said. "How do you feel?"

"A little better," she said. "Thanks for bringing down your yesterday's clothes."

"That's okay." Jerry dumped them into the clothes hamper. "You should've stayed in bed, Mom," he told her. "I can fix my breakfast."

"I'm up now," she smiled. "I might as well fix it. Eggs and toast?"

"Yes, please." He watched her crack the eggs into a pan and scramble them. He got two slices of bread and dropped them into the toaster.

"Your father said that you didn't do so well last night," said Mrs. Steele.

"I didn't do well at all, Mom," Jerry said.

She smiled at him. "You've got to work harder."

"I will, Mom," he said. "I promise."

Jerry hoped that he'd see Danny Weatherspoon before the next game, but Danny seemed to be keeping out of sight. Jerry was worried. Had the little guy lost faith, believing that Jerry would never listen to him?

I hope not, Jerry thought. *I really hope not.*

While he was putting on his uniform in the dressing room, a shadow crossed in front of him and paused. Jerry looked up into Freddie Pearse's unsmiling face.

"Tell you what, Jerry," Freddie said. "If you play, I'll give you a dime for every basket you make. For everyone you miss, you give me a nickel. Fair enough?"

"That's gambling," Jerry said. "Sorry."

Freddie snickered. "Why don't you admit that you don't have a chance to win?"

Jerry rose from the bench and stood with his face within three inches of Freddie's. "Because I do, Freddie," he said evenly. "I have a very good chance."

122

He strode out of the locker room, feeling Freddie's eyes boring into his back.

The game was against the Pilots, and Jerry didn't get in till the second quarter. He saw the familiar stone-hard expression come over Freddie's face and wondered if, after the game was over, it would be gone. He would just have to wait and see.

The Pilots played well. Jack Horn, their center, was an equal match to Freddie, and now and then seemed even better. He scored seven of the Pilots' eleven points during the first quarter, while the Chariots racked up nine.

"Okay, Jerry," Coach Stull said. "Let's see what you can do."

Fresh and full of vitality, Jerry went into the game with the worst scoring record he had ever had, and began to play as if it were his best. Sparking the guys with chatter whenever he saw their spirits waver, the team regained new vigor and played like a brand new ball club. The score was tied 31 – 31, with two minutes to go in the first half, and Jerry had yet to take a shot.

Finally, when Ronnie passed to Jerry near the basket, and no one was near him — Jerry shot.

His heart still, Jerry turned and watched the ball strike against the boards, bounce back, roll around the rim, and drop *in*.

A resounding cheer exploded from the Chariot fans as Jerry rushed downcourt to cover his man. He thought of a little guy with an elfish smile and looked up at the bleachers. There sat Danny, clapping his hands and shouting, "That-a-boy, Jerry! You've done it! Keep it up!"

Jerry thought he detected more than one meaning in that last sentence. Yes, he promised himself, that's what he would do. He would keep it up, doing his chores at home to lighten the burden for his mother and father, and being obedient and honest to them and to his teachers and friends. He might have to put a lot of effort behind all this, but the rewards on the court and off would be great.

He watched a Pilot bring the ball up-court, then he quickly shifted as the Pilot started to throw a pass. Instead, the play faked him out of position and the Pilot tossed to another man.

Disgusted for momentarily having been fooled, Jerry raced after the receiver. But the man had taken a step toward the basket and shot, and the ball sank through the net for two points.

"You didn't look hot on that play, man!" Freddie laughed.

Jerry ignored him, trying not to show the puzzled look that came over his face, for suddenly he was uncertain again about whether or not his promise to be an honest human being to his parents and friends would mean anything.

Again the thought came to him: *Is Danny a warlock, or isn't he?*

Three seconds before the clock on the scoreboard ticked away the first half, Jerry stole the ball from a Pilot, dribbled up-court across the center line and shot. The ball arced high through the air, dropped, and slithered through the hoop with barely a whisper. The buzzer sounded just as the crowd let out a loud, ear-piercing yell.

"Should've bet with me, Jerry," Freddie said in the locker room as the boys wiped their faces with towels and sucked on orange slices. "You would've made twenty cents."

Jerry grinned. "No, thanks, Freddie. Even if I were sure of hitting every shot, I wouldn't take you up on it."

"Why not?"

"I told you. I don't gamble."

A hand patted him on the shoulder. He turned and saw the smiling face of Coach Stull. "Nice shooting, Jerry. Looks like you're back in the groove."

"There's still another half to go," Jerry said.

When the second half started, Jerry was in there, playing as hard as he had that second quarter. His dribbling and passing fired up the Chariots, and the team moved in front of the Pilots, 47 – 39. His own shooting was next to spectacular, but not perfect. Twice his set shots missed, but three of his lay-ups went in, and so did two foul shots out of three.

In the fourth quarter he kept up his pace, scoring a shot now and then, passing to Ronnie or Freddie who, in turn, would shoot — sometimes missing, sometimes hitting. He kept watching the expression on Freddie's face as the minutes dragged on toward the climax of the game, and with each minute he saw a change. After a while, kinder remarks came from Freddie's lips. "Hey, you're shootin' like wild, man!"

"Where'd you find your eye, buddy?"

"Good play, Jerry! You're really cookin' with gas!"

When the game ended the victorious Chariot fans let out a cheer, a kind that hadn't been heard in a long, long time.

Hands pounded Jerry's back and shoulders, and happy words thundered in his ears.

"Jerry, I'm glad to see that you're back in your old form again," Coach Stull said, beaming at him as they shook hands.

Freddie Pearse shook his hand, too. "I used to be jealous because you scored more baskets than me," he confessed. "Then I got sore because you weren't hitting 'em at all."

Jerry smiled. "How do you feel, now?"

"Darn good. I like winning, no matter who scores the most baskets."

"Thanks, Freddie."

Jerry looked around for another face, saw it, and his heart pounded. Danny Weatherspoon ran up to him, his grinning face radiant, his eyes shining brightly.

"I knew you'd finally come through,

129

Jerry!" he cried. "I knew it all the time!"

Jerry's eyebrows lifted. "You knew that I'd finally start sinking shots again?" he asked.

"That — yes," Danny said. "But I'm thinking about you and your promise. Your mother and father will be real proud of you, Jerry. Just as proud as I am. Now I'll be able to go back to Salem and give a good report."

Jerry frowned at him as he turned and started away. There was still doubt in Jerry's mind.

Suddenly Danny turned and his eyes sparkled. "By the way, it was nice of you to have fixed your own bed this morning, even if you didn't do a good job."

Jerry stared at him. "How did you know about that?"

Danny grinned elfishly.

"Then you really *are* a warlock!" Jerry exclaimed.

Danny winked. "Isn't that what I've been telling you all the time?" he said.